214975

For Graham
RI

For Helen
MK

Rose Impey has become one of Britain's most prominent children's story tellers. She used to be a primary teacher and still spends much of her time working with children.

Moira Kemp is a highly respected illustrator. When illustrating The Creepies she drew heavily from her own childhood experiences.

First published in 1989
by Ragged Bears Ltd
Ragged Appleshaw
Andover, Hampshire SP11 9HX

ISBN 1 870817 07 9

Designed by Herman Lelie
Produced by Mathew Price Ltd
Old Rectory House
Marston Magna
Yeovil BA22 8DT
Somerset, England

Printed in Singapore

Creepies

The Ankle Grabber

Rose Impey

Illustrated by Moira Kemp

RAGGED BEARS LTD

Every night
when I go upstairs
my mum has to check out
the whole room
before I get into bed
and turn off the light.

First she draws back the curtains
to make sure that
The Flat Man
isn't hiding there
pressed back
against the glass
ready to slide out
and get me
when the light goes off.

Then she looks carefully
through the wardrobe
in case Jumble Joan
is hanging there
soft and lumpy
pretending to be
a harmless set
of old clothes.

And last of all
she gets down
on her hands and knees
to search for
The Ankle Grabber,
who lives in the invisible swamp
just beneath my bed.

Even when Mum tells me
'It's all clear,'
I can never be quite sure.
I peep round the door
then make a quick dash
and jump on to my bed
from the middle of the room.

I try to keep well away
from the grabbing hand
which might shoot out
any minute
pulling me
by my ankles
down
down
down
into the sticky swamp
never to be seen again.

Then I pull the covers
up to my nose
and peep over them
around the room.

My mum shakes her head.
She says, 'I've told you before,
there aren't any monsters
in this house.'
Then she kisses me goodnight
and goes downstairs.

I lie in bed
all alone
in the dark
and my head
feels full of monsters.

I think of The Chimney Creeper
and The Guitar Gobbler,
but most of all
I think about
The Awful Ankle Grabber.

I think about
its two greedy eyes
rolling
like glass marbles
from side to side
in its hooded head.

They peer out
above the swamp
always on the lookout
for anything
which might fall its way.

And I think about
its grasping hands
with their lizard-like fingers
reaching out
on long scaly arms
to get me.

I picture them
curling their fingertips
as they climb
up the side of my bed

creeping nearer
and nearer until they are
almost touching me.

I shiver
and squeeze myself
as thin as I can
into the very middle of the bed.
I tell myself,
if I stay there
without moving
I will be safe.

The Ankle Grabber can't get me
because it's stuck
in its slimy swamp.
No matter how much
it stretches
and struggles
it can't get out.

And I picture it
sinking back
into the mud
which boils and bubbles
round its ears,
sucking it down

until only two glassy eyes
are left,
waiting and watching
in the dark.

I turn over
and over
rolling myself up
in the covers
like a huge swiss roll.
I hate it
lying there
wide awake
with my head full of monsters.

Then another horrid thought
creeps into my brain.
I start to think
I want to wee.

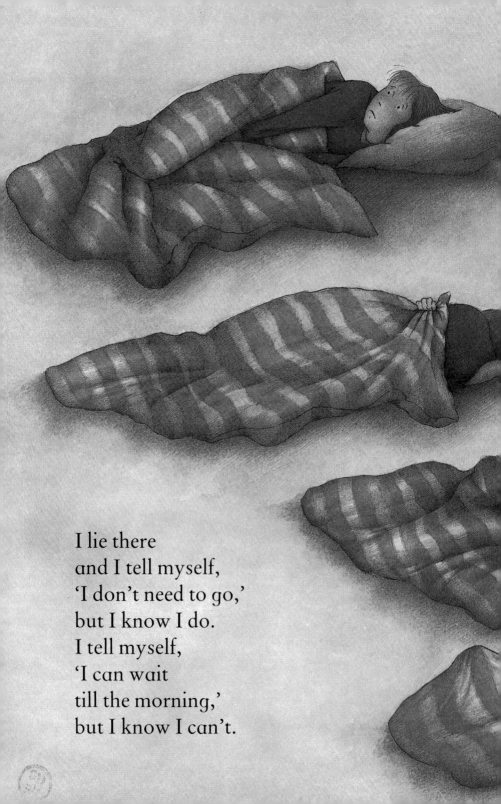

I lie there
and I tell myself,
'I don't need to go,'
but I know I do.
I tell myself,
'I can wait
till the morning,'
but I know I can't.

I try to think about
something else
but all I can think of is
rain
and waterfalls
and dripping taps
and in the end
I know I've got to go.

I take a deep breath
and make a jump
in the dark.

I land softly
near the door,
tiptoe along the landing,
and have a wee.

Then I make a run
all the way
from the bathroom

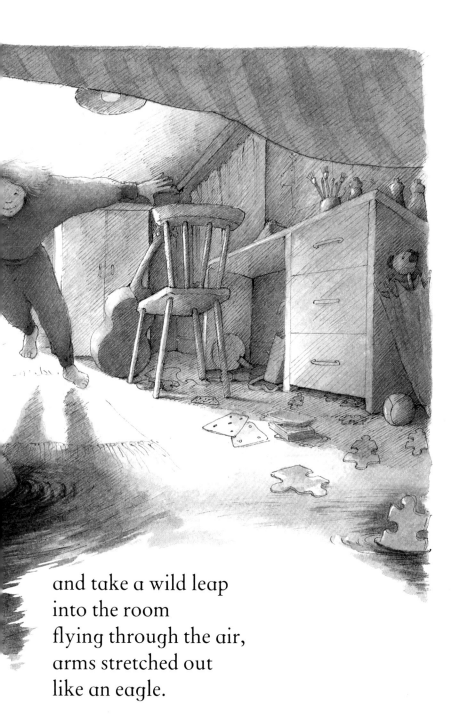

and take a wild leap
into the room
flying through the air,
arms stretched out
like an eagle.

But I miss.
I hit the floor
with a BANG

landing face down on the carpet
with my head
almost under the bed.

I hardly dare to look
in case I see
The Ankle Grabber
watching me.
Any minute his scaly hand
could shoot out and grip hold of me.

But then, when I do look,
I see someone else's eye
staring back at me.
My teddy's sitting there
on top of the swamp.
I reach out
to save him
before he is sucked in
and lost forever.

Suddenly I stop dead.

Behind me
I can feel a large hand
cold and rough
closing around my ankle.

It grips me hard and pulls me
with a sudden WHOOSH!

I feel myself sliding
along the bedroom floor.
I start to scream,
'Help! Mum, Dad! Help!'

'Now what are you doing
down there?' says my dad.
I lie on my back
looking up at him
feeling pretty silly.
'I thought you were
The Ankle Grabber,' I say.

'Oh, it's The Ankle Grabber tonight,'
says Dad. 'Not The Terrible Toe Twiddler.'
'No,' I say, 'not him.'
'And The Nasty Knee Nibbler,
he hasn't been back?'
'No,' I say. 'You scared him off.'

'Then it sounds to me
like another job
for The Dreadful Demon Dad.'

'Look out,' I call.
'My Dad's coming to get you!'